DREAMWORKS

VOLTRON
LEGENDARY DEFENDER

Space Mall

Adapted by Natalie Shaw

Simon Spotlight

New York London Toronto Sydney New Delhi

This book is a work of fiction. Any references to historical events, real people, or real places are used fictitiously. Other names, characters, places, and events are products of the author's imagination, and any resemblance to actual events or places or persons, living or dead, is entirely coincidental.

SIMON SPOTLIGHT
An imprint of Simon & Schuster Children's Publishing Division
1230 Avenue of the Americas, New York, New York 10020
This Simon Spotlight edition December 2017
DreamWorks Voltron Legendary Defender © 2017 DreamWorks Animation LLC.
TM World Events Productions, LLC. All Rights Reserved.
For information about special discounts for bulk purchases, please contact Simon & Schuster
Special Sales at 1-866-506-1949 or business@simonandschuster.com.
Designed by Jay Colvin
The text of this book was set in United Sans Reg.
Manufactured in the United States of America 1117 LAK
2 4 6 8 10 9 7 5 3 1
ISBN 978-1-5344-1022-0 (hc)
ISBN 978-1-5344-1021-3 (pbk)
ISBN 978-1-5344-1023-7 (eBook)

CHAPTER 1

Ten thousand years ago, Voltron was piloted by five original Paladins. One of those Paladins was King Alfor, Princess Allura's father. Another pilot, the Paladins had just learned, was Emperor Zarkon.

Zarkon had flown the Black Lion, making him the original Black Paladin. It was through this connection that he was able to track Voltron—and attack the lions. If the Paladins were to have any chance against

Zarkon, Shiro would have to form a new bond with his lion.

"One that's stronger than his," Shiro said.

Meanwhile, Coran and the other Paladins needed to get new Teludav lenses for the Castleship. Their lenses had recently broken. Without them, they couldn't travel via wormholes and had even less of a chance of escaping Zarkon's next move.

"I think I may know where we can get some," Coran said. He showed everyone a picture of a swap shop run by the Unilu space pirates.

"Coran!" Allura protested. "You're not suggesting going to one of those filthy swap moons? The last time you went, those space pirates took you for everything you had."

Coran smiled, lost in thought. "Of course you had to bargain," he told the Paladins. "No one could bargain like the Unilu. Now, let's ready a pod for our mission."

"Shotgun!" Lance shouted, and ran at full speed to get the pod's front passenger seat.

"What? No, you have to be in the hangar to call shotgun!" Hunk said, running after him.

Meanwhile, Shiro climbed into the Black Lion's cockpit.

"You and I have some work to do," he said. "What do I have to do to strengthen our bond?"

Suddenly, the doors to the hangar opened, and the Black Lion took off! Shiro and the Black Lion raced into space at the speed of light.

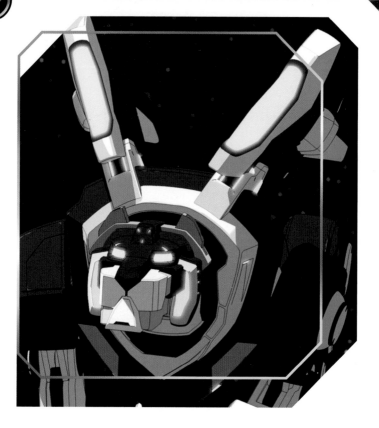

"Stop. Stop! Turn around. That's an order!" Shiro shouted. He tried to jam the controls to force the lion to listen to him, but the lion just kept flying.

When it began to slow down, Shiro looked out and saw a burnt-out husk of what was once a planet.

"What are you trying to tell me?" Shiro

asked the lion. Then the lion's eyes began to glow. Shiro took this as the lion wanting him to see through its eyes. He closed his own, and let the lion take over.

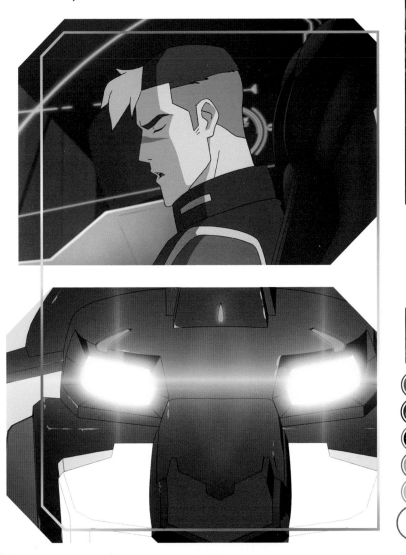

With the lion's eyes, Shiro saw visions of a vibrant planet with thriving cities. When Shiro opened his eyes again, the planet was in ruins once more.

"Was this your home?" Shiro asked, though deep down he knew the answer. He was visiting the remains of planet Daibazaal, the planet on which the Black Lion had lived with Zarkon.

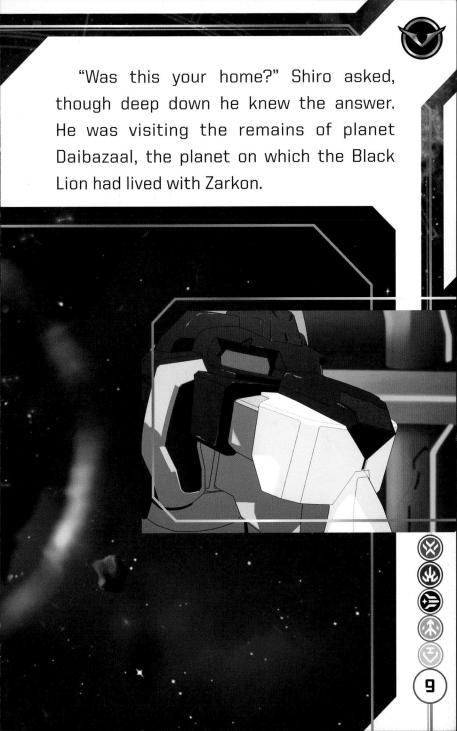

CHAPTER 2

Coran prepared the Paladins by giving them disguises as they approached the Unilu swap moon. Soon Coran, Pidge, Hunk, Lance, and Keith were all dressed like space pirates!

But upon entering the Unilu market, they felt out of place.

"Uh, Coran?" Pidge said. "This looks an awful lot like a regular mall."

It was true.

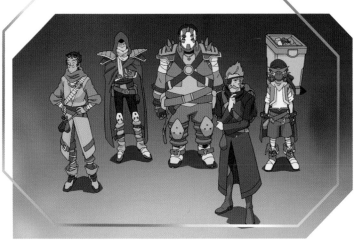

"It does seem to be a little *cleaner* than I remember," Coran admitted. There were multiple floors overlooking an atrium, escalators, and wide halls lined with stores. It was definitely a space mall. "Still, be vigilant. The Unilu are cutthroat wheeler-dealers. So keep your hands on your coin satchels."

"My satchels are empty," Hunk said.

"Good," Coran replied. "Everyone, let's fan out and search the area for Teludav lenses. We'll meet by the giant ticking clock here in one varga. Don't be late, and try to blend in!"

Little did the Paladins know, up in the security center, a space mall cop was digging into take-out food and watching them on a monitor.

"Space pirates!" the mall cop shouted, throwing his take-out container aside.

The guard watched as the Paladins took off their disguises and threw them in the trash, revealing their regular clothes.

"Disguising yourself as harmless shoppers, huh? Well, it won't work," he said, getting the wrong idea. Then he went to his locker to grab his gear, and gazed lovingly at the picture of Zarkon that was taped inside.

"Don't worry, Emperor Zarkon," he said. "I know you can't be here to protect the mall, but your faithful number two is on the case. Time for the pirates to face Varkon."

Following Coran's orders, the Paladins split up.

"If I were a ten-thousand-year-old wormhole lens, where would I be?" Hunk

asked himself. But he was soon distracted. There was space food, and it wasn't the same old space goo on the Castleship! He entered a food court filled with strange delicacies.

"This. Is. Beautiful," Hunk said. "Maybe the Teludav is under these samples." He took a

bite of a green tentacle from a sample tray.

"Mmm, rubbery!" he said as he chewed.

Next, he tried a fried snack.

"Ooh! Sweet and salty," he said.

He gulped down a drink. "So cold." He shivered. Then his face turned beet red. "But spicy."

A purple alien held out a tray of unappetizing purple globs.

They tasted as bad as they looked.

"Eh. What's next?" Hunk asked, unimpressed.

The alien held out his hand, demanding payment.

"Sustenance provided by Vrepit Sal, that's me. Five hundred GAC is now owed." His name was a clever play on words of the Galra greeting, *Vrepit Sa!,* but he didn't seem to have a sense of humor.

"I thought this was a free sample situation," Hunk explained.

"Free?" Sal didn't seem to understand.

"Look, I don't have any money, so . . . ," Hunk began. Before he could finish his sentence, Sal chained him to a sink full of dirty dishes in the kitchen.

"Oh man," Hunk whined, and looked around at the others who were in the kitchen. "How long have you been here?"

An elderly blue alien was scrubbing dishes on the floor.

"Sal put me in when I was just a little girl," she said.

Hunk began to wash dishes sadly—and dream about escaping—as a robot chef mashed a bunch of food together into a pile. When it was ready Sal pulled on a string and an air horn blew loudly.

"Forty-three!" Sal yelled, and passed the plate to customer number forty-three.

"Sustenance unit complete," Sal ordered. "Ingest."

The customer looked at the disgusting brown glop and sighed.

Suddenly, the robot chef short-circuited and collapsed. A red *X* appeared on its indicator screen.

"Not a*gain*," Sal said. "Now who will be my sustenance preparer?"

"I got this, Sal. Uncuff me," Hunk volunteered. "Trust me. I'm an enthusiastic gourmand with an incredible palate. Also, your robot is dead."

Sal couldn't deny that. He moved Hunk's chains so that he could be near the stove. "All right. Work!"

A ticket order came in. Hunk tried to read it, but it was written in another language. "Doesn't matter. I'll improvise," Hunk told himself. He put together a beautiful-looking plate of food and showed it to Sal. "Do you smell how the tanginess of the tuber mash really brings out the charred flavor of the palmagoren filet?"

Sal nodded and reached to pull the string, but Hunk stopped him.

"Let's just say 'Number forty-four? Your order's up!'" Hunk said cheerfully. An alien walked up to the counter. "Enjoy your meal," Hunk said.

The alien took a bite. Instantly, she was in food bliss. It was her favorite thing she'd ever tasted. "Mmm!" she said, and smiled.

"What did you do to her face? It's cracking!" Sal shouted.

"She's *smiling*. She's enjoying her food," Hunk explained.

Sal smiled now too. He grabbed the next order slip and gave it to Hunk.

"Okay. Let's provide some sustenance!"

CHAPTER 3

While Hunk was revolutionizing Vrepit Sal's kitchen, Keith stumbled upon a stand that sold specialty knives. Something had been bothering Keith recently. He had been given a blade in his youth that had an emblem similar to one of the Galran rebels they'd met some time ago. Keith didn't know why a blade with a Galran symbol ended up with him on Earth. But perhaps the salesman might know.

The salesman was in the middle of a demonstration.

"Let me show you the wonderful workings of the Galasu X-90 Extreme Blade System," the salesman said, twirling knives in two of his four hands. "It slices, it dices, it slaughters and skins, and it constantly stays razor sharp. Look at it cut through this bloato fruit!"

He pulled out a round, green fruit with his bottom set of hands and threw it into the air. With his top hands he effortlessly used two knives to cut it into paper-thin slices as it fell to the cutting board.

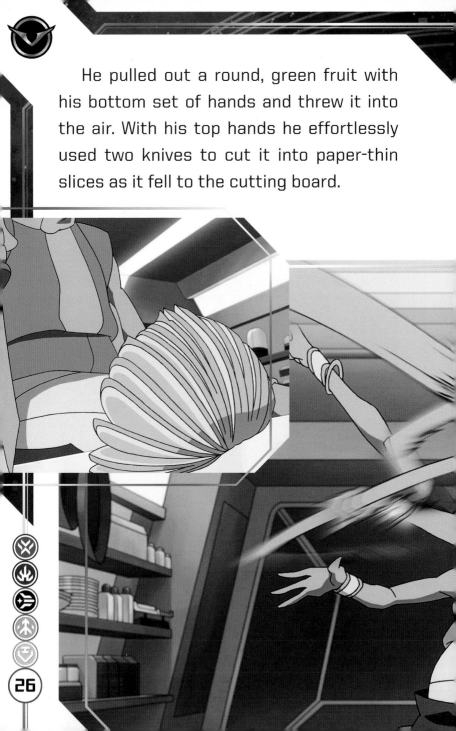

"But wait, there's more!" the salesman continued. "How many times have you had to fight off a charging rock monster and then go immediately to a picnic? All the time, right?" He used the knife to cut through a giant rock— and then cut the bloato fruit. "How much would you pay for it? Seriously, how much?"

The other customers walked away. Keith was impressed, but he had no intention of buying a knife.

"I just had a question," Keith said. "Have you ever come across something like this?" He placed his blade on the table.

"Whoa," the salesman said as he inspected it. "This craftsmanship is incredible. And is this a Luxite blade? The planet they mined that from hasn't existed

in deca-phoebs! Where did you get this?"

"Someone gave it to me," Keith said.

"That's vague. Tell you what, I'll give you a thousand GAC to take it off your hands. No, two thousand!"

"It's not for sale," Keith said, but the salesman yanked it off the table.

"How about this? I keep the knife and

you beat it before security gets here. I know it's stolen," he threatened.

"It's not stolen," Keith insisted. Then he grabbed the knife and ran off.

"Hey! Come back!" yelled the salesman. He pressed an alarm.

Up in the security center, trusty space mall cop Varkon heard the alarm ring.

"Trouble at the Slice Capades?" he said, pulling up some surveillance footage. "It's one of those pirates! Varkon's coming for you!" He booted up his hoverbike and rolled out into the mall.

Meanwhile, Shiro was still aboard the Black Lion by Daibazaal's remains, strengthening their bond. The Black Lion was showing him images of its past.

"Show me more," Shiro said. When he closed his eyes, he saw a comet crash into Daibazaal. Then he saw King Alfor get the comet out of its crater . . . with Zarkon's help. Next he saw King Alfor unveiling the lions, which he had created with material from the comet, and Zarkon becoming the Black Lion's Paladin.

"King Alfor built you from that comet. And you fought beside him. With Zarkon," Shiro said to the Black Lion.

Then Shiro gasped as, in the vision, Zarkon stared directly at him.

"You!" Zarkon snarled.

Back at the space mall, Varkon saw the huge line at Vrepit Sal's. "What's going on here?" he wondered, and scooted closer to investigate.

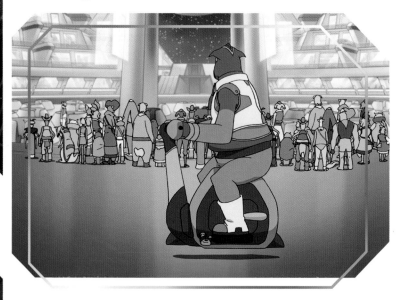

At the food stand, he heard a voice shouting orders. It was Hunk.

"I said over *medium*!" Hunk yelled, holding a plate of food in front of Sal. "Does this look over medium to you?"

"No, Chef," Sal said.

"Then let's get it right," Hunk said,

chucking the food in the trash. "If it ain't perfect, it ain't coming out of this kitchen!"

Hunk expertly drizzled sauce on another delicious-looking meal and turned to present it to a customer. "Bon appétit."

But instead of a customer, Hunk was face-to-face with Varkon!

"I got you now, pirate. Where are your friends?"

"Uh-oh!" Hunk said, and hopped over the counter. "Don't forget what I taught you!"

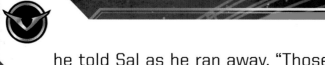

he told Sal as he ran away. "Those are the fundamentals of cooking!"

Sal shook his head. He was a changed alien.

"That kid is a genius. I don't care if we have to search the entire galaxy. I want him back at Vrepit Sal's," he vowed, watching Hunk escape.

CHAPTER 4

"Can I interest you in the latest Earth fashions?" an alien shopkeeper asked Lance. The shopkeeper was dressed head to toe in Earth fashions—if he were about to star in an Earth rap video, that is!

That's when Pidge spotted them. "Lance, we have to be back at the clock in a half hour."

"But, Pidge! Look at all this crazy Earth stuff," Lance begged.

"We're supposed to be looking for Teludav lenses . . . ," Pidge trailed off, but then her eyes lit up. She spotted a video game console on display. "Oh my gosh. Mercury Gameflux II with the original power glove that gives you infinite lives if you touch the index finger to the pinkie? We have to have this! How much is this?"

"Twelve hundred GAC," said the shopkeeper.

"Is that a lot?" asked Pidge.

"Compared to what we have, which is none? Yes, it's a lot," Lance quipped.

Pidge and Lance left to find some money.

"Don't sell that," Pidge told the shop-keeper as they walked away.

"Don't worry. I never sell anything. Do I, Kaltenecker?" the shopkeeper said to a cow behind him.

"Mooooo," said Kaltenecker.

Pidge and Lance splashed around, barefoot, at a wishing fountain in the mall. They were just short of the twelve-hundred-GAC asking price when an alien tossed a coin into the fountain.

"Already on it!" Lance screeched, and caught the alien's coin with his teeth.

Pidge and Lance cheered. They'd done it! They had twelve hundred GAC! They returned to the store and bought the video game console.

"With every purchase you get a free Kaltenecker," the shopkeeper said. He handed them a leash. It was connected to the cow he was talking to earlier.

That's when Hunk and Keith ran by.

"Security is on our tail!" Keith said, pointing at Varkon, who was gaining on them.

"Ah!" screamed Pidge. She and Lance
ducked out of the store—with Kaltenecker
behind them—and ran as fast as they could
throughout the space mall. But then they
came to a dead end.

"Everyone up on Kaltenecker!" Lance
commanded.

"Did you buy a *cow*?" Hunk asked.

"It was free with purchase!" Pidge explained.

They all hopped on Kaltenecker's back, ready to escape.

Back in the Black Lion, Shiro saw another vision. This time, the Black Lion sprouted huge, feathered wings.

"Those wings! You have powers I haven't unlocked," Shiro realized.

In the vision Zarkon flew the Black Lion toward an alien ship. It looked like they were about to crash when the lion disappeared . . . only to reappear on the other side of the alien ship. It had teleported!

Incredible, Shiro thought.

Then Zarkon seemed to stare right at Shiro again.

"I've got you now, Paladin," Zarkon told Shiro.

Suddenly, the space between Shiro and Zarkon collapsed and they stood across from each other on a kind of mental battle-field, with the Black Lion sitting between them.

"You are a fool to face me here. When you die in this realm, your body dies as well. And then I will take control of Voltron!" Zarkon yelled.

Armed with only their brute strength, they began to attack each other. Shiro fought hard, but Zarkon was more powerful. Shiro was in trouble.

CHAPTER 5

Meanwhile, Coran stumbled upon a real, old-fashioned Unilu shop. It was piled with what looked like junk. It was exactly what he'd been looking for!

A Unilu greeted him. "This shop's been in my family since before the empire began. Can I interest you in a butcher barrel or perhaps a set of window breakers?" he asked.

Coran spotted a set of Teludav lenses.

"Teludav lenses, yes!" Coran said quietly,

but then tried to play it cool. "I mean, I don't have any idea what these pieces of junk are."

"I see you've got your eye on these antique glass table toppers here," the Unilu replied.

"Well, they're pretty ugly, but I do have an empty curio cabinet for grotesqueries. How much do you want?"

The Unilu squinted at him. "How much have you got?"

"I have a handful of pocket lint," Coran said.

"I'll take your firstborn child," the Unilu replied without missing a beat.

"I might be able to throw in a used hand-kerchief," said Coran.

"I could accept your left foot," said the Unilu.

"I would be willing to sing you a song."

"You become my butler for one year."

"Two Altean crown bills," Coran offered.

"Five Valuvium ingots," the Unilu countered.

"Would you accept an IOU?" Coran asked.

"Of course. I'll just need some collateral. Maybe *ten* Valuvium ingots," he said, doubling the price.

Coran pulled out an Olkari Cube from his pocket. "How about this?" he asked. That did the trick.

"You've got a deal," the Unilu said, taking the cube and giving the lenses to Coran.

Coran walked out of the shop victorious—and found the Paladins riding Kaltenecker. He jumped on.

"You can't pilot the Black Lion after everything you've done," Shiro said to Zarkon. "You can never lead Voltron again. You're *no* Paladin!"

Re-energized by his own speech, Shiro hit Zarkon. He was back in the fight!

"You have no idea how to command a weapon like this," Zarkon sneered.

But Shiro had learned something important.

"No one commands the Black Lion," he said.

"You dare lecture me?" Zarkon threatened Shiro. Zarkon and Shiro fought each other fiercely. Zarkon was right. What

happened to Shiro's body in the mental realm happened in the physical, too—inside the Black Lion, Shiro was injured, and his life was in danger. On the mental battle-field, Zarkon picked up Shiro by the neck and held him in the air!

"Do you think the Black Lion would allow such a feeble creature to pilot it?" Zarkon sneered. "Only the powerful can command it."

"It's not about power. It's about earning each other's trust," Shiro told Zarkon, straining to speak.

"Trust has nothing to do with it. That lion is mine. Forever."

As Zarkon squeezed Shiro's neck even more tightly, the Black Lion's eyes began to glow. It had heard everything. It agreed with Shiro.

The Black Lion opened its mouth and blasted Zarkon with an energy beam, pummeling him back to his own ship and back to reality.

"My connection grows weaker," Zarkon realized, back on his Galran ship.

Meanwhile, Shiro woke up in the cockpit of the Black Lion.

"Did you just save me?" he asked the Black Lion. But he already knew the answer—the Black Lion had. "Let's go home."

The Black Lion didn't move. Instead, its background started shifting and shifting. Shiro looked around and realized they were in the Black Lion's hangar.

"We never left," Shiro said, amazed.

Coran and the Paladins raced outside the mall, with Varkon close behind them. But Varkon stopped at the door. He couldn't follow them outside.

"Don't let me catch you in my jurisdiction again, pirates!" Varkon yelled.

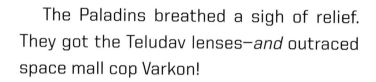

The Paladins breathed a sigh of relief. They got the Teludav lenses—*and* outraced space mall cop Varkon!

Back on the Castleship, everyone greeted Allura.

"We got our lenses," Coran announced.

"Excellent," Allura said. "Now we can get the Teludav up and running."

"Where's Shiro?" Keith asked.

The door opened, and Shiro came walking up, looking a bit dazed. He glanced to his right and saw Kaltenecker behind Lance.

"Is that a cow?" he asked.

Kaltenecker mooed.

"So, did you find a way to bond with your lion?" Keith asked Shiro.

"Yes, and we need to get moving," Shiro said.

Now that they had the lenses, there was no time to waste.

While Coran plotted their next course—a

mysterious base of alleged Galran rebels—
Pidge and Lance went to set up their new
video game console.

Pidge pulled out the video game console
and looked around, holding the old cables in
her hand. She searched for an outlet. Then
it dawned on her.

"Where can we . . . How do we . . . *No!*"

Pidge's eye twitched.

There was nowhere to plug it in!

The Space Mall!

Greetings, pirates. Can I interest you in the latest Earth fashions?

My name matters not, but I am the shopkeeper at It's Earth, located in the space mall. Please do come in. Take a look around. I have the finest collection of Earth items in the whole universe.

Over to the right you will notice a large metal object called a "car." This is like a spaceship that doesn't fly and doesn't go into space. I'm not quite sure what it's for, but rumor has it that earthlings use their cars as an outlet of expression with various bumper stickers. I've seen cars with bumper stickers of babies and honorary student awards. It's a bit out there, but you know the humans!

Toward the back of my shop you will find two rare palm trees. Humans grow these hideous plants in warm weather, like on the island of Cuba. I suppose someone from

Cuba would be excited to see them—excited enough to stop in and take a look around the shop, anyway.

My hat, in case you were wondering, has the number "51" on it. Area 51 is a place on Earth where I go to get the latest fashions. It is located in a place called Nevada, and I always make sure to stop by a nearby city called Las Vegas for a second or two. Nobody has noticed I'm an alien there yet.

Aha! I see that you have your eyes set on Kaltenecker. Worry not! One free Kaltenecker comes with every purchase. He makes the best milkshakes in the universe, but don't ask me how to milk him. Now, what can I assist you with today?